Romance Me or Not

POETRY FROM THE HEART

By Angela Hugee

aka Lady A in the world of poetry

DEDICATION

This book is dedicated to everyone that has experience true love on the highest level, on the lowest level, as well as to those that has never experience true love at all. I pray that until you find it, you will experience a sample of what true love taste like with every verse that you read. True Love is a recipe of many emotions and experiences. It's seasoned with compassion, intimacy, hurt, disappointment, joy, pain, triumphs, trauma, drama, lost, gain and many other ingredients that life throws at you, with the most important ingredients being God.

Romance Me or Not

ISBN: 9798336757118

ACKNOWLEDGMENTS

A special acknowledgment to all the people within my inner and outer circle that has impacted my life in various ways. Rather it was a positive or a negative impact, it all contributed to the woman I am today and for that, I want to say Thank You.

TABLE OF CONTENTS

Walk With Me

Walk with me, as I walk.
Talk with me, as I talk.
Sing with me, as I sing.
Dance with me, as I dance.
Love me, as I Love.

My Life Without You

My life without you would be meaningless,
Not worth living at all. My world minus you,
Would truly crumble and fall.
The air I breathe without you
Would not be healthy for me to inhale.
Each breathe I take without you
Would be, like poking holes in my throat with nails.
The sun would not appear as bright,
without you in my life.
The stars would not shine in the sky.
There would be no day or night.
The rain would not even phase me,
Because I would be to numb to know,
That I was getting wet or frost bitten from the snow.
I would not be able to comprehend,
a word, that's spoken from someone's mouth,
Because I would be lost minus you,
Trapped in a maze with no way out.

I would not be able to talk
Because I would be too frail and weak.
Much words to say but without you to hear me,
For what reason shall I speak?
My eyes would have cried a river,
And I would be drowning in the tears,
my eyes had produced.
A death that I wouldn't want to be rescued from,
Because my life would be meaningless without you.

you are my happily ever after

Silly of Me

Silly of me thinking
That if I come to you,
Like a woman
Express how I feel,
like a woman
You won't dismiss me
like a child
So you can pout for a little while.
I didn't attack you
I didn't smack you
I didn't accuse you
I didn't disrespect you
All I did was ask you.
And instead of addressing it
You decided not to talk to me.
So, now it's in me that,
I can't talk to you
About things that are on my mind
Because if it offends you,
my concerns become minimized.
And click, you'll be gone,
not saying goodbye,
Just hanging up the phone.
Silly of me thinking
That if something bothered me
It would bother you too
And we would talk it out
Like TWO real grown adults do.
Silly of Me, Thinking.

A Computer Love Virus

A virus got into my computer one day
And somehow got into my mind.
It infected my soul so quickly, instantaneously,
in no time.
It entered in through my finger tips
And seeped quicky through my veins.
Up my arms, into my heart and mind,
This virus, boldly came.
It seeped throughout my body rapidly,
Giving me no time to delete it.
Before I could lift my fingers off of the key board,
The damage had been completed.
I thought viruses only infected computers.
Went after computer parts.
But I wrong, for this was a **love virus**
And without warning, it (you) had captured my heart.

More of YOU

I have an unlimited amount of space in my heart, in my mind, in my body and in my soul for YOU. YOU fill me up daily, yet I'm not full. I'm always craving more of YOU.

More conversations, more text messages, more emails, more flirting, more visits, more time alone, more time to do everything, more time to do absolutely nothing, more time to share food, more overpacking, more cuddling and more intimacy.

YOU satisfy me completely, in every way. YOU and your love I could never, ever get tired or enough of. I'll always crave and want More of YOU.

Thank You

Thank You so much for entering into my life at the time (I didn't know) I needed you the most. Years of abuse, being hurt, being let down and disappointed had led me into decades of safeguarding my heart. I guarded it so well, that when it came to a relationship, you could have all of me, except my heart. I could show love with limitations but being truly in love was off limits. It hurts letting someone in my mind and near my heart because the outcome was always the same.

When I met you, I had the urge to run but Thank You for holding on to me with all of you might. Thank You for burying my feet into your invisible concrete and for not letting me go. I promise you; I am worth it. I promise you, that I am worthy of you. I promise you, that I am worthy of your love.

Thank You for breaking through my invisible, emotional wall without physically breaking through. My heart is aching without hurting and it's ok because that means it's still beating. That means that it is capable of loving You and ready to be loved by You.

If I Only Knew

If I knew this was going to be the last time,
I got to see your face,
I would tell you how much I love you,
how your presence lights up my space.
If I knew this was going to be the last time,
that we went for a walk,
We would go on an endless nature trail and just talk and
talk and talk.
If I knew this was going to be the last time, that we spent
together,
before we forever depart,
I would savor every minute, etch and engrave them in
my heart.
So, treat every minute like it's the last time.
Love and enjoy those close to you,
before you be waking up tomorrow saying,
If I Only Knew.

I Am Poetry

From the way that I smile
From the way I hold my lips when I talk
From the tone of my voice
Down to the stride in my walk.

From the way I cover my mouth when I laugh.
From the way my voice sounds when I speak.
From the flaws in my skin
Down to the gap in my teeth.
I Am Poetry and Poetry is Me

From the words that I write
From the way those words rhyme
From the way I express who I am
Down to the way, together, these words sound

From the clothes that I wear
From the shoes on my feet
From the style of my hair
Down to my writing technique
All of the above attributes
Are what makes me unique
I Am Poetry and Poetry is Me.

Out of Sight, Out of Mind

Out of sight, out of mind
A statement to me that is not to clear.
Because even when you're not with me,
In my mind, you're always here.
Just because you're not here with me,
Doesn't mean that I don't think of you.
The way you smile, the way you smell.
The way you glaze at me the way you do.
Just because you're not next to,
doesn't mean that you're not here.
For I can hear your laughter,
I can feel your touch,
I can feel your passionate kisses,
That gives me such a thrill.
Out of Sight, Out of Mind,
there's no truth to that statement, I say,
because even when we're not together,
you'll in my thoughts, Always.
You might be Out of Sight,
but you're never Out of Mind.

I'll Never Forget

All my life, I've waited for YOU.
With YOU in my life,
my gray skies are now blue.
My soul now skips to the beats
that my heartstring sings.
Tears falling from my eyes,
equivalent to a nice summer rain.
My mind constantly replays the day we met
50 plus years later, I'll never forget.
YOU touched me,
before YOU ever physically touched me.
By your side is where I always want to be.
I felt YOU before YOU ever caressed me,
releasing trapped in emotions, setting them free.
I Loved YOU, from the moment we met,
50 plus years later, **I'll Never Forget.**

I Don't Like You

My heart races when you call.
I answer but don't let you through.
My soul rejoices when I hear your voice.
Yet, I Don't Like You.

My blood boils when I see your smile
and my pulse flutters like a kite.
this wall around me is slowly crumbling
that's why, it's you, that I dislike.

My smile goes from ear to ear
and my cheek bones sometimes crack.
My emotions bubbles as if they're about to erupt
yet, again, it's you that I don't like.

Our time together, yet apart is priceless.
It has me wishing that time could stall
I want to tell you how much I'm missing you
But I Don't Like You at All.

You Are A Book

You are Love. You are Loved. You Are a Book, a Story waiting to be told. Find love within yourself. Find Love within your own Book. Find Love within your own Story. Then, find someone that wants to read Your Book. Find someone that wants to become a part of Your Story. Find someone that Loves You, then together, create a new story, together write a new book.

Stop Settling for the Settlement

We want to see more than what there is,
so we remain in situations, where no hope lives.
Never receiving,
but consistently we give.
Trying to turn a piece of coal
into the most valuable gold.
Expecting to make sweet tea,
from a sour lemon tree.
Trying to take a sip of water from a well run dry.
Trying to surf the waters
When there is no tide.
Trying to substitute whip cream,
with shaving cream.
Trying to turn a stripper
into the lady of your dreams.
Trying to mold a man, to fit your mold.
Trying to turn a hand full of rocks,
into a pocket full of gold.
We got to stop settling for the settlement,
Believing that something,
compared to nothing is best,
When in reality we're only
short changing ourselves.

Make yourself a priority

Don't Disturb My Peace

Don't come for me and disturb my peace
If you know you're not ready for all of me.
I pray to God for discernment,
to show me what I cannot see.
To make things more visible to me.
Like your lies, your deceptive ways
Smiling and grinning all up in my face.
Pretending to be searching for something steady,
When you knew all along that you weren't ready.
So, when I walk away from you,
I will hold my head up high, eyes dried,
Not one tear for you, will I cry.
All I have for you is a wave goodbye,
for coming for me, trying to disturb my peace,
knowing that you weren't ready for all of me.

Don't Disturb

My Peace!

Let Me Be The One

Let Me Be The One you come home to
after you've labored all day long
and after your workday is through.
Let Me Be The One you can talk to and trust,
Open up to and share what's on your mind.
Knowing that whatever you tell me,
I will always be by your side.
Let Me Be The One that helps to ease your pain,
massaging your body from head to toes.
Attending to your every need,
comforting all your woes.
Let Me Be The One to undress you,
and run the water for your shower.
Let me be that soap that lathers you,
and afterwards, let me be the towel.
That wraps warmly around you,
comforting you for hours.
Let Me Be The One, to love you.
Satisfying all of your needs.
And at night, let it be my arms that holds you,
Before you fall asleep.
Let Me Be The One.

LOST IN YOU

I get so lost in YOU without being lost.
Miles of rivers to find YOU, I had to cross.
When I'm with YOU, I can tune out the world
without tuning out life.
I can taste YOU without taking a bite.
I drink YOU in without taking a sip.
I can taste your love as I lick my lips.
With YOU, I'm floating in the air yet my feet remain on
the ground.
I can still feel your presence even when YOU are not
around.
YOU make My heart skip, flip and sing,
yet in my chest cavity it remains.
My Love for YOU, mere words can't capture how I feel
It's a Love so powerful, if I wasn't experiencing it,
I would wonder if it was real.

I Will Always Feel This Way

As I look into your eyes,
I feel so much love seeping through.
Reassuring me more than ever,
That all of my life, I've waited for you.
As I place my arms around you,
Holding you as tight as I possibly can,
My heart softly but loudly whispers,
Yes, you are that man.
As you gently kiss my lips,
I can feel our passion burning greatly.
A feeling that I've never known
But with your touch, you manage to generate it.
So, when I then tell you that I Love You
that my love for you grows stronger every day,
just know that without a doubt,
I will always feel this way.

Flipped A Switch

Until you, my emotions and body
were in a frozen state.
Just meeting you,
the ice slowly started to melt away.
You touched my hand
And the ice instantly dissolved.
It felt as if your hand reached into my soul
And flipped on a switch.
A switch that enabled me to feel and to love.
Thank you for igniting a fire,
within me,
That now burns constantly
Within my soul.

Takes My Breathe Away

As you tell me of your love for me,
I yearn for and need you more.
And with each detail of how you'll love,
I begin to shimmer beyond control.
As you speak of how you'll pull me close
I hunger for your caress.
I patiently away, though on fire inside,
as I rest my head upon your chest.
With every thought of how you would love me,
I become eager to explore.
Wanting the thoughts to stop because you are not here,
Yet my body is begging is more.
As I think about our first kiss,
our first touch, our first long, embracing hug,
it satisfied me completely,
Without you being here my love.
I anxiously await for that day to come,
When we can be together, always.
Just thinking about how satisfying
that moment will be,
Takes My Breathe Away.

With You and Missing You

I miss you when I'm with you
and I miss you even more when we are apart.
You've set camp in my mind and soul
and vastly making a home in my heart.
When I'm with you I just want to be close to you
memorizing and absorbing how you smell and feel
so when I'm not with you all I have to do is close my eyes
and vision that you are here.
When I'm with you I'm always wishing,
that time will just creep by.
And when I'm not with you, waiting to see you,
I wish that time could fly.
When I'm with you I feel like this is where
I am supposed to be
and when I'm not with you I feel so lonely
because you are not here with me.

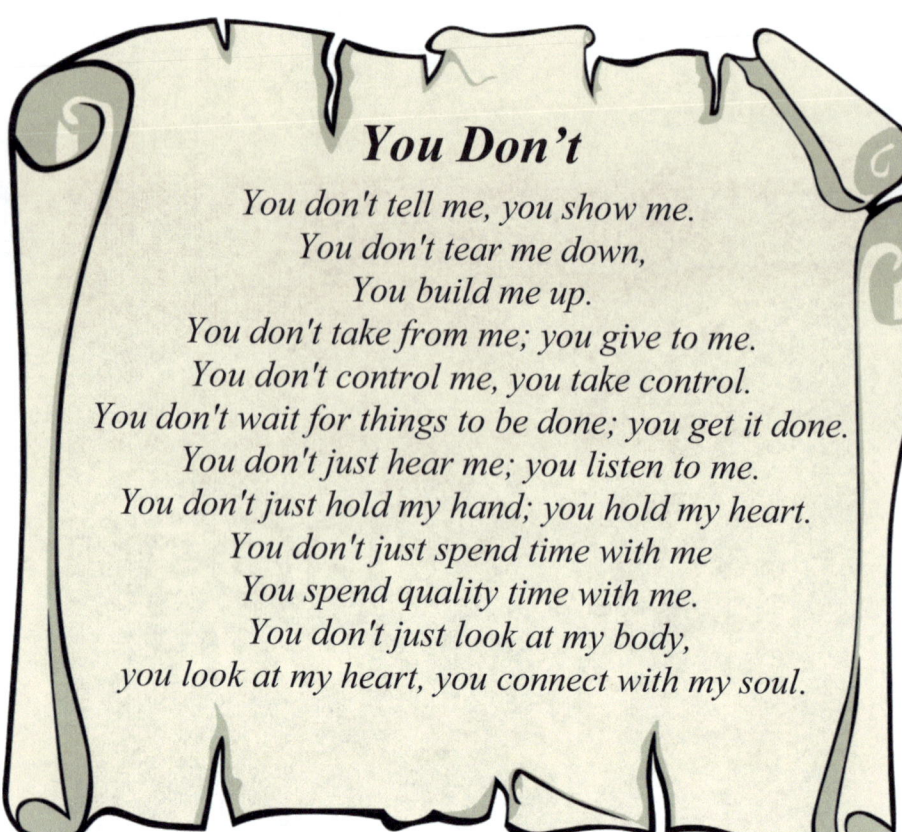

You Don't

You don't tell me, you show me.
You don't tear me down,
You build me up.
You don't take from me; you give to me.
You don't control me, you take control.
You don't wait for things to be done; you get it done.
You don't just hear me; you listen to me.
You don't just hold my hand; you hold my heart.
You don't just spend time with me
You spend quality time with me.
You don't just look at my body,
you look at my heart, you connect with my soul.

I Loved You….

I loved the way YOU looked at me,
Before YOU ever saw me.
I loved the way YOU caressed me,
Before You ever touched me.
I loved the way YOU wrapped
your arms around me,
Before YOU ever held me.
I loved the way YOU pressed
your lips against mines
Before YOU ever kissed me.
I LOVED YOU, before I ever
I knew, that it was
YOU, that I LOVED.

I've Waited for This Moment

I've waited for this moment,
for a very, very long time.
Not knowing what to expect
Has bought confusion to my mind.
I am very eager and overly anxious.
Excited, overjoyed and intrigued.
Not knowing exactly how you'll feel about me,
Causes weakness to my knees.
My heart is beating so rapidly,
Pounding like a drum major,
playing his drums in a band.
I'm so nervous, I'm shimmering,
Can't seem to steady my shaking hands.
I've anticipated this moment
over and over in my mind,
and now that the occasion is arriving,
I feel I need more time.
I wonder if we close our eyes,
would I feel you and you feel me?
Would we feel the love and attraction
between us,
before each other's face, we do, see?

Would we feel the burning passion,
that dwells within each other's heart and soul?
A passion that is so powerful,
A fire that will never grow cold,

I Could Never Find

I could never find a love so warm
Nor do I plan to seek.
For your love is so hot, it burns.
It's like walking on hot sand, barefoot, on the beach.
I could never find a love so pure.
So unconditional, so heartwarming, so true.
No reason for me to seek perfection,
For all I need, I have in you.
I could never find a love so real,
As the love that we share.
A love so binding, so electrifying,
A love that doesn't need words, only a stare.
I'll never stop telling you that I Love YOU.
What a treasure you are, a priceless piece of art.
How you've painted everlasting memories,
That hangs forever in my heart.
I Could Never Find.

Special Without Being Special

I got home and sipped on some wine.
Got real comfortable then put on some jazz to unwind.
I sat back and kicked up my feet.
Before I knew it, I was fast asleep.
I fell asleep still embraced in your hug.
Still smelling your smell as I, in and exhaled,
I could still feel your presence there.
So thank you for the brief moment we share
It was such a delight.
It was special without being special.
It was the highlight of my night.

Hold Me MyLove

As I lay here waiting to fall asleep
your handsome face is all I see.
I can feel your arms holding me tight.
Oh, what comfort it brings me through the night.
I can still taste your lips on my lips.
I'm absorbing every gentle, yet, passionate kiss.
Hold me MyLove, Never Let Me Go
it's YOU, that my soul, desires the most.

I Have Yet

I have yet to see your lovely face
But I vision it every day.
I have yet to hear your lovely voice
But engraved in my heart are all the beautiful
Things, to me, you're going to say.
I have yet to glaze into your eyes
But I'm quite sure I'll be able to see straight through
Into your heart, mind body and soul,
Seeing all the love for me, that dwells, in you.
I have yet to hold your hand,
I have yet to feel you hold me in your arms,
but you've already swept me off my feet,
with the thoughts of your loving charm.
I have yet to kiss your lips
and savor your wonderful touch
but I'm positive, that I won't be disappointed
because I already Love the thoughts of you so much.

If I Close My Eyes Real Tight

If I close my eyes just a little,
I can feel you breathing heavily on my neck.
If I shut them even tighter,
I can feel the warmth of your body, closely pressed.
As every second passes by,
I can see on your forehead, beads of sweat.
I can feel your arms around me.
I can feel you pulling me close.
I pull away as if I'm not into you,
When in your arms is where I want to be the most.
When I shut my eyes even tighter,
I can feel you kissing and holding me.
At that moment, there is no place on earth,
that I would rather be.
And just before I fall asleep,
with my eyes still shut tight.
I can hear you whisper in my ear,
I Love You, dear, **goodnight.**
With my eyes close I can imagine and pretend
That you are here whenever I want you to be.
The imagine is so real sometimes,
that when I open my eyes, I'm shocked to see,
that you are not here with me.

Before I Met YOU

I thought that the love I had for YOU
Over the weeks might flicker and die.
But it has only acquired the wings of an eagle
And to new heights, each day it flies.
I was wondering if our love was true
Or just a vivid imagination of my mind.
But every time I search my heart,
It's YOU, that I find.
I was wondering if someone was worthy of me loving
with all my heart, body and soul.
But that was before I met YOU
For you are worthy of all my love and so much more.
I thought I would never fall in love.
Never experience the joy and passion that being in love
brings.
But then YOU came into my life,
and I now feel and know all of these things.
I thought no one would ever love me,
Igniting in me a fire too hot to be true,
Loving me with all of their heart, body and soul,
but that was before I Met YOU.

When I Love

When I love I really love hard
but I'm always getting played like a broken guitar.
Trying real hard to find the right note,
sounding like I'm entangled in a musical stroke.
Just because I love you,
doesn't mean that I won't walk away.
Just because I love you doesn't mean I'm here to stay.

All My Life

All my life I dealt with
Peep who did me wrong.
Peep who treated me wrong.
Convinced me I was wrong
Took me for a ride
You're not my ride or die.
More like my suicide.
Bad choices after choices
Beating me like a gong.
I didn't bring mistakes,
mistakes were bought along.

More Time

I've liked you from a distant
I've admired you from afar
With every text you send me
You're slowly seeping in my heart.
I think about you constantly
You're always on my mind.
If I could, I would
add a few more hours to each day
Because I feel I need more time.
More time to think about you,
imagining that you are here with me.
Because in your arms,
right by your side,
is where I ALWAYS want to be.

As I Close My Eyes

It's 2 o'clock in the morning and I can't sleep
Thought of you in my mind playing hide and go seek.
Like a tidal wave, flooding my brain,
mini visions of you, falling like rain.
As I close my eyes, all I can see,
Is me lying in your arms and you holding me.

Mysteries of the Heart

The heart is very mystical.
It feels joy, it feels love, it feels pain.
It endures so much emotions,
Ofttime losing more than it gains.
The heart is to be handle with much gentleness.
It should be labeled fragile, handle with care.
Be caution of how you deal with it,
Its contents you must beware.
For the heart contains many emotions and feelings
And can easily be shattered like glass.
Destroying all that is within it,
sometimes, beyond repair.
So if I give my heart to you,
would you tend to it,
as if the blood flowed from your veins?
Or would you misuse and abuse it?
Being not concern about the damages it might sustain.
For my heart is very fragile
And should be handles with a gentle touch.
So will you be my shield and protect it,
preventing it from being crush?

P.S. Note to Self
(be prepared for true love when it comes knocking)

I really do get scared sometimes, okay, most of the time. Just when I feel the need to lace up my running shoes, a little voice inside of me whispers, who are you running from and why?
Me:
I'm running away from myself.
I'm running away from being hurt again.
I'm running away from the way you make me feel, which is happy and loved.
I know, who runs away from feeling happy and feeling loved? (I do)
But, one day, I'm going to listen to that little voice inside of me that's telling me to let him in, let him love you and if you love him, just love him.
It really can be that simple.

I Can't

I've heard never say what you Can't do
because it's such a negative word.
But to me and in my heart and mind,
it's one of the most powerful words I've ever heard.
I've always been told say and thing I can,
It's more of a positive statement and this is true.
But when it comes to expressing my love for you,
the words I Can't, is the only ones that will do.
For I can live my life without you
but I Can't live without you in my life.
I can do without a lot of things,
but you, I Can't do without.
I can always find another lover,
but I Can't stop loving you.
No man will ever have my heart,
the way that you do.
I can be with another man,
but in love with another man, I just Can't be.
I Love You, heart, mind, body and soul.
You mean the world to me.

I can think of other people,
but I Can't stop thinking about you
and how you came into my life,
Giving me a love so real, so true.
So I prefer the words I Can't.
Because it describes so much of what I do.
With the number one and most important being,
I Can't Stop Loving You.

So, I Silently Whisper

*My heart, harbors and safeguards all that my mouth is
afraid to say,
for fear that once it's verbalized, the beauty, would fade
away.
My heart, so full of love, anxiously anticipates.
While my soul fears the feeling might dissipate.
Once it's shared, once the words are spoken out loud,
Would the beauty remain, or vastly evaporate in the
clouds?
For I can text the words I Love You
And every letter of every word would be true
But I fear the fear of my heart being broken,*
So, I silently whisper *I Love You, to You.
And not because I don't, because every fiber of my body
do.*

Shame On You

You come for me you better come straight
cus I can read your mind like a magic 8,
BALL,
bouncing off the wall,
your mine so dazed you're about to fall,
into your own tangled web that you have weaved.
Meant to trap me but I broke free.
Why do you take so much pleasure in trying to deceive,
the hand that fed you,
protected you,
at night, caressed you.
Fool me once, shame on you
Cus I'm not sticking around for round two.

Your Smile

You take my breath away
every time I see your smile.
I just want the world to stop,
so I can linger there for a while.
Absorbing all the rays,
that your smile displays.
No matter the season,
your smile is the reason,
that I smile from within
captivated by all the joy,
your smile brings.

Who Are You?

Who are you that has swept me off my feet?
Every time you call me, my heart, it skips a different beat.
I had no idea that it would have been you
But it was instantaneously, from the moment your voice
came through.
My love for you, one would say is insane
for the happiness I feel, I myself can't comprehend.
Could it be because I've finally found a mate, a lover, a
friend?

At This Very Moment

At this very moment,
I was thinking of you and I began to smile.
A chill ran up and down my spine
and it lingered there for a while.
I was standing in my bedroom, cleaning for the day.
When all of a sudden, I felt your presence
in a breeze that blew my way.
Where did that breeze come from?
When all the windows and doors
were closed as tight as they could be.
I don't know but what I do know is,
it bought much joy to me.
I turned around to touch you,
for I thought you might be there.
But all I found was an empty space,
around me, everywhere.
A single teardrop ran down my face
and I felt you kiss it away.
I heard you whisper in my ear,
we'll be together soon baby, soon, one day.
So, I'll just continue to smile,
Whenever I feel your presence near me.
And one day soon, when I turn around,
there to stay, my love, you will be.

You're Always There

Not a single day goes by
without me having you on my mind.
Not even an hour passes by,
without me wishing that you were all mines.
You're on my mind every minute.
Every second of every day.
Even in my dreams,
my thoughts of you are not misplaced.
Even in my nightmares,
I vision you standing there.
You're even in my daydreams,
it's of you, I sit and stare.
You're even in my prayers,
before I get in bed and fall asleep.
How can I not love you,
when you're always here with me.

**You are intertwined with my spirit, you dwell in
my mind and you have set camp in my heart.**

Only You

If there's a man in this work that can make me smile
and is half as sweet and nice as you.
He must be a wonna be or your clone,
Even then he couldn't make me feel the way that you do.
If another man came into my life
And tried to invade your space.
He would be the last man in a marathon,
For he would truly lose this race.
If another man tried to capture my heart,
telling me all the wonderful things for me, he would do.
He would be fighting a losing battle,
Because my heart, already belongs to you.
It another man tried to sweep me off my feet,
He'll need a street sweeper to perform that task,
Because my heart is already anchored and cemented,
And in you, is where it's at.
It doesn't matter what's placed before me.
If you're not part of all of the above,
for In my heart, there's no room for another man,
because it's you, that I Love.

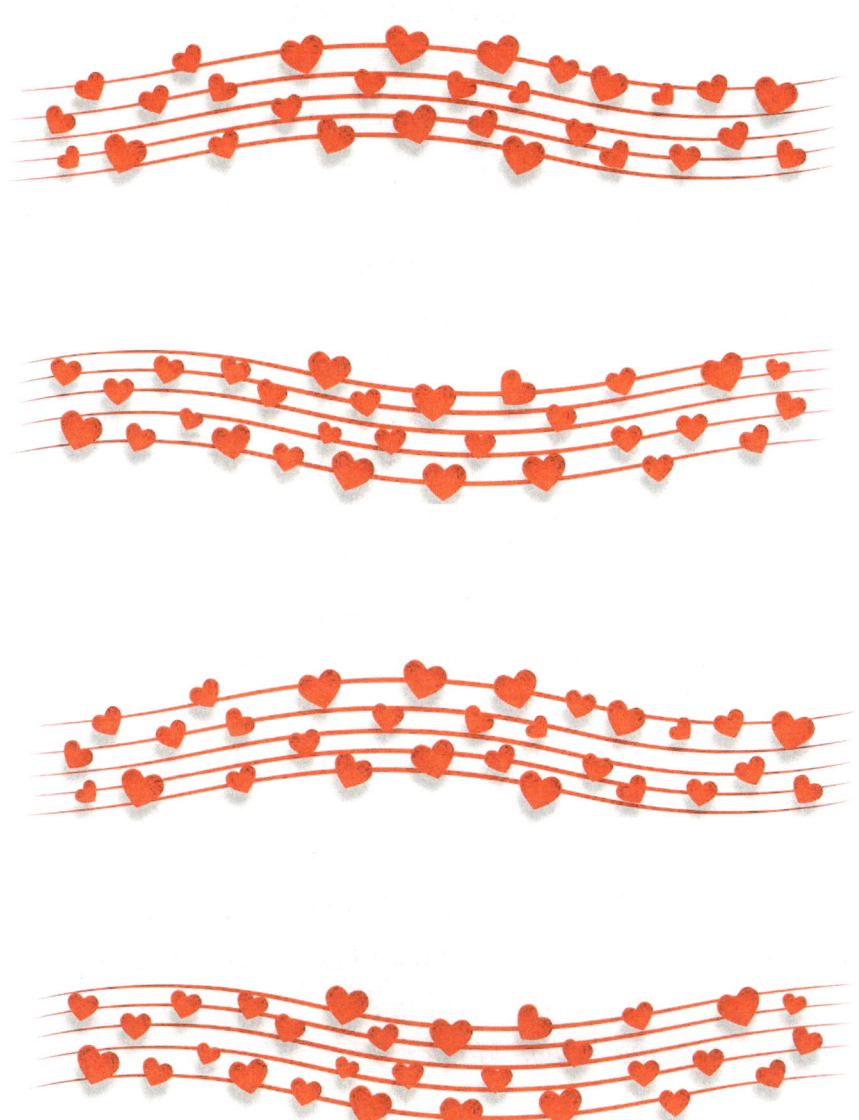

Close To You

I want to be so close to you.
Closer than your mouth kissing my lips.
Closer than your hands gripping my hips.
So close, that I'll know how many times your eyes are blinking.
Close enough to know what your mind is thinking.
I want to be so close to knowing and loving you.
So close that only my love will do.
So close that when your heart is aching,
I will be that pump, that prevents it from breaking.
Closer than the warmth that an electric blanket brings.
Close enough so that I will be able to hear your heart sing.
Close than your chest, pressing against my breast.
Closer than the pillow, that you lay your head on to rest.
So close to your body, closer than your skin.
So close that your heart will never break again.
I want to be so close that there's no need for you to be calling.
For I will feel when you need me and I will be there,
in an instant,
To comfort you, my sweet darling.
So Close.

I Don't' vs I Do

When I tell you that I don't like you,
I really want my (not like you) to be true.
Because I'm trying to save myself from pain,
I struggle with I don't vs I do.
I'm trying to shield myself internally,
so that my exterior emotionally walls
won't be exposed.
Because if I relax, just a little,
you would enter in, my locked,
keyless, entry door.
It's so much safer for me to believed that
you don't like me,
instead of believing that you do.
Because when you walk away,
my world won't fall apart.
Yes, I said when, because they always do.

Tears of Joy

A tear of joy rolled down my cheek
Followed by a tear of pride.
Several tears of happiness soon followed,
For all the love for you, I have inside.
A tear of missing you managed to escape
No matter how hard I tried.
Soon tears of needing you also broke free,
Before I knew it, I had begun to cry.
Then tears of loneliness seeped out my eyes
And I tried real hard to flutter them back.
But it was too much for me to control,
At that moment, strength, was something that I lacked.
Finally, a smile came on my face,
As I thought of how much I Love You
In spite of it all.
So, although I cry a lot of times,
*It's mostly **Tears of Joy**.*

I Was Thinking

I was thinking that if I touched you,
you would surely disappear.
So I kept my hands to myself
because I wanted to keep you near.
I was thinking that if I gave you a kiss,
which was something that I wanted to do,
that you would have pushed me away
and I didn't want to be rejected by you.
I was thinking *that when the clock struck 12 am,*
I would be all alone.
That if I turned over and reached for you,
My Cinderfella would be long, long gone.
I was thinking that when I awoke,
When morning finally came in,
I would not find you by my side,
That being with you was only a dream.
But when I reached out to touch you,
you hadn't left, there you stayed.
When I leaned in to kiss you,
You did not push me away.

And when the midnight hour came,
You were still with me.
And there was no other place on this earth,
that I would rather be.
Then when morning finally arrived,
There by my side, there you lay.
So, I snuggled as close as I could next to you,
Praying that it will always be this way.

Sometimes

Sometimes I just sit and stare,
Hearing your voice in my ear
And wishing that you were here.
Sometimes I just sit and cry, whenever I hear your name,
But I don't know why.
Sometimes I just imagine that you are holding me close
because in your arms is where I want to be the most.
***Sometimes**, I just sit and smile, thinking about you*
Makes the bad times worthwhile.
Sometimes when I go to bed at night,
I pretend that you are my pillow
And I'm holding you tight.
Sometimes.

You're Always With Me

I did not get to see you today,
though I visited you in my mind.
Even though we seldom spend time together,
you're with me all the time.
You walk with me every day,
You're always in my dreams.
You are so much a part of me,
my only reason for existing,
it sometimes seems.
I hate it when I don't get to talk to you.
For without you here,
your voice is all I've got.
I know that I have your heart
but talking to you means an awful lot.
I sometimes feel like I can't go on,
living like this, with us being apart
but how can I live my life without?
When you have possession, of my heart.

On The Day That You Were Born

On the day that YOU were born,
a new star appeared up in the sky,
capturing the eyes and hearts of everyone that saw it,
because it (YOU) sparkled with such pride.
On the day that YOU were born,
In an unexplainable way, so was I.
Although it has taken us many years to find each other,
The wait was worth it, just to look into your eyes.
On the day that YOU were born,
I never imagined, never knew,
that YOU would come into my life
and I would love YOU like I do.
On the day that YOU were born,
the world became a better place for me
because YOU became a part of my world,
before we ever did meet.
On the day that YOU were born,
a new star appeared up in the sky,
capturing the eyes and hearts of everyone that saw it,
and now that I've met YOU, I know why.

I Loved You Before

I loved you before you were conceived.
I loved you before your birth.
I loved you before ever knowing you.
I loved you before you first step on Earth.

I loved you before I met you.
I loved you before I knew your name.
I loved you before we ever talked,
and now that we have met,
I love you just the same.

I loved you before I ever saw your face.
I loved you before we ever touched
and in spite of us just meeting,
I love you, oh, so much.

Do We Share the Same Dreams

When did it start?
And when will it end?
Or we destined to be husband and wife,
Or just passing friends?
You said that we would be friends for life
but that doesn't mean that I would be your wife.
I wanted a friendship, a marriage
all that I thought I had in you, something strong
but perhaps the dream I was dreaming
was wrong all along.
I was feeling so overwhelmed,
Because I was thinking that
all my wants, needs and dream had come true.
All that I ever wanted (flaws and all),
I thought I had in you.
But by dreaming the same dream,
won't make a dream come true,
unless the person in your dream,
is dreaming the same dream as you.

The Greatest Love of All

While I was out today,
My mind was focus on YOU.
I was thinking about all the talks we've had
And all things we have yet to go through.
I was thinking about when we met.
When I first walked out that red door.
From the moment YOU first spoke to me,
I couldn't ask for anything more.
I was thinking about just being in your presence.
Sharing the same air that YOU breathe.
Just to look into your eyes,
Puts my mind at ease.
I was looking at other couples holding hands,
thinking, no way they could be happier than You and I.
No way that they can say I Love You,
just from feeling each other's vibe.
No way that they can, generate an electric spark,
every time they get together.
No way that their hearts beat as one,
No, no other love could be better (than ours).
For the love we share is the greatest of all.
A Love That Will Last Forever.

I'll Never Take You For Granted

I will always treasure you being in my life
And I'll always let you know.
You are like rain falling on my tiresome body
It's because of you that I smile and glow.
I will always say thank you, you're welcome
And ask you how was your day.
Compliment you for the littleBig things you do,
Giving your mind no time or room to stray.
I will never take for granted,
That you are always there for me, whenever I call.
Or how you are my human trampoline,
Always there to catch me when I fall.
All of our time together
Will be more spectacular than the day before.
With all the new ventures and different avenues,
That together we will explore.
Communication would become
Our closest and best friends
Always sharing what's in our heart
To the very end.
I'll Never Take You For Granted

There's a lot that is good in your life—don't take it for granted. Don't get so focused on the struggles that you miss the gift of today.

-Joel Osteen

I Give You All of Me

There is so much in life that I want to give to you. I want to give you the moon and all the beauty that it portrays as the day slowly turns into night. With the moon in your grasp, you will always have a light to direct your path wherever you are in life. But, because giving you the moon is impossible, I would love you, all of you, unconditionally, from your insides out. From your head to your toes, creating a glow within you that would shine externally, guiding you in the direction that you would need to go. **I Give You All of Me**

If I could, I would reach into the sky and grab a handful of stars and place them all around you so that your eyes will always have that sparkle and shine whenever I look at you. But, since the stars are out of my reach, I would become those stars and sparkle and shine all around you, all over you, shining all through you so that you can feel my love shining from within you and even when we are miles apart, you will know without a doubt how much I Love You. **I Give You All of Me**

I will never be able to physically move Heaven and Earth to make you happy and to satisfied you but I can make you feel like you are in Heaven, every day that you are here on Earth. **I Give You All of Me**

The hours in a day, I can never change. I can't make the hours go by any quicker nor can I make time stand still but what I can do and what I'm willing to do for you is spend every second, of every minute, of every hour, in every day making sure that you know how much I Now and Always Will Love You. So, it won't matter how fast or how slow time passes by because when we are together, it would be, Time Very Well Spent.
I Give You All of Me

Ride or Dine

(together, we will survive)

When I'm hurting and all I can do is write.
Constantly Praying to God that he will make it right.
God, please help me make it through the night.
Because this is a battle that I cannot fight. (alone)

I love YOU and all I want to do
Is be the best woman that I can be for YOU.
I've told YOU that I'm your Ride or Dine.
Whether we drinking tap water or sipping wine.
YOU can take that to the bank cus I ain't never lied.
Trying hard to be strong when I wanna cry.

In my heart and soul, God led me to YOU,
So, I know that God will see us through.
I know Challenges, we are going to face.
It's not how the battle started
it's about how we finish the race. (together)
All I know is I Love YOU and I hold on that
Because in YOU is where my heart is at.

When I'm hurting and all I can do is write.
Constantly Praying to God that he will make it right.
God, please help me make it through the night.
Because this is a battle that I cannot fight. (alone)

Beauty Lies In the Beholders Eyes

I was like a dying, withering rose,
Starving for water and light to survive,
when you entered the garden and picked me,
and I am still wondering why.
When there were so many other
Flawless and beautiful roses
that you could have chose,
but you came along and picked me,
the unworthiest of all the rose.
My leaves were dry and brittle,
While the other roses leaves
were green and shined.
My petals had nearly all fallen off.
I was not worth a dime.
My thorns were even useless.
They were too dull to pop a ballon.
But you took me home and nourished me,
causing me to bloom.
You placed me in the nicest vase,
watered me, and placed me in the light.
You tended to my every need,
Morning, noon and night.
You took something that was dying,
All you saw was what I could be,
When I, myself had given up on living,
And you bought back life to me.

It's because you watered me,
that I began to grow.
It's because of your touch,
my beauty, I now, show.
I now stand tall and radiant,
generating back to you some of that light.
It's because of all the love you've shown me,
That my petals, now shine so bright.

I'm Sorry

I'm sorry that I sometimes don't think before I speak.
That I never view YOU as being weak.
When things hurt me and make me cry,
I use YOU as my handkerchief to wipe my face dry.
You soak up all of my tears, collecting them one by one,
Absorbing my sorrows like a sponge.
Am I so blind that I cannot see,
That you're also crying, only silently.
And when I'm lonely from missing you,
How can I not see that YOU miss me too.
My pain, I constantly place in your eyes,
While your pain, though not intentionally, I minimize.
When knowing in my heart, that YOU Love me and I
Love YOU,
I should know that whatever hurts me, hurts YOU too.
Just because I wear my heart on my sleeve
That doesn't mean that your heart don't bleed.
I wish YOU were here so that I could apologize
And kiss away your invisible tears
And return to your face, that handsome smile.
I hope that in your eyes, the next time YOU look at me,
That woman you fell in love with, is still who you see.
I'm sorry for causing YOU to be upset with me,
For only acknowledging I'm in pain, instead of we.

*So please forgive me for the thoughtless things I
sometimes say and do,
And give me the opportunity to make it up to YOU.
For without YOU in my life, I don't know what I would
do.*
I'm Sorry.

I Want To Share With You

There's so much I want to share with you,
Because of the way you make me feel.
I want to show you how much I care for you,
so that you'll know that my love is for real.
There's so much I want to tell you.
So much I want to say.
I want to share my innermost thoughts with you,
Now and Always.
I want to share your joy, your pain.
I want to share your ups and your downs.
I want to get to know all of you.
What makes you smile, what makes you frown.
I want to share in your laughter.
Wipe away your tears when you cry.
I want to share my life with you,
Because I Love You, that is why.

If I Give You My Heart?

If I give you, my heart,
Something I've never given to anymore before,
would you return that love,
or would you walk right out the door?
(With My Heart)
If I give you my heart,
with all of the damages it has sustained,
Would you look pass all my scars
and only see, all the joy,
to you, that I would bring.
If I give you my heart,
would you shield it from all aches and pain,
promising to protect it,
so that I won't ever be hurt again?

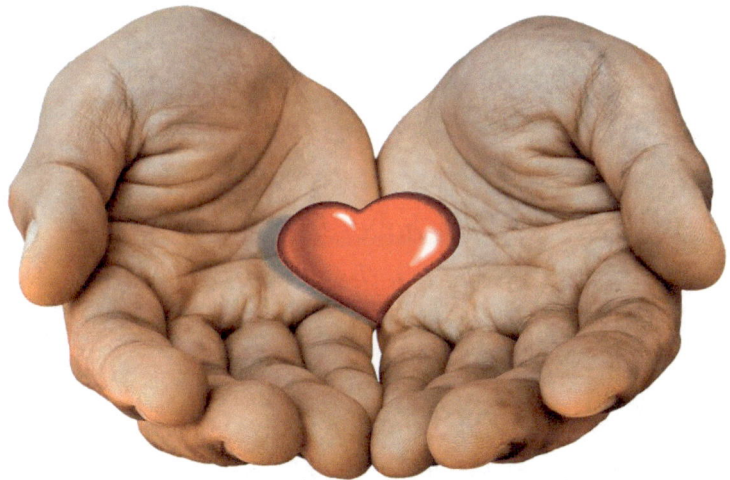

My Knight In Shining Armor

I had never experience true love,
and I never knew that there would come a time,
when YOU would enter into my life, becoming my
personal ray of sunshine.
Your love is like the sun ray.
YOU bring comfort to me day and night.
Where I go, there YOU are,
shining on me like a spot light.
Every time YOU look and smile at me,
I feel like I'm a star, sparking bright.
How honored I am,
that you reached in the sky and picked me,
when there were millions of others stars in your sight.
YOU make me feel like I'm a movie star.
On stage, with all eyes on me.
A princess taken out of a fairy-tale book,
My prince, YOU will always be.
My Knight in shining armor,
the only True Love for me.
From the moment you shined into my life,
I knew, I would love YOU, for eternity.

A Love So Addicting

Your love is very addicting.
It keeps me coming back for more.
Your kindness is hypnotizing.
Your sweetness, I adore.
Of YOU, I could never get enough.
You're like some kind of drugs.
But none I need to get high off.
I'm high off of your love.
You keep a smile upon my face
And much love for YOU, in my heart.
I believe, without me knowing it,
I Loved YOU, right from the very start.

My Life Minus YOU

My life minus YOU
Would be like the wind blowing,
without a breeze.
Or, me, trying to take a walk,
through a forest without trees.
I would be driving around in a car,
minus all four tires.
Lost in a maze, with no way out
because it's you, that my heart desires.

My Once Simple Life

You've stirred up feelings in me,
That I didn't know was alive.
Feelings that are scaring me,
bringing me joy, yet making me cry.
I was happy, content with my life,
before you entered in.
Now my once simple life,
will never be simple again.
What am I feeling? I do not know,
so many years have come and gone.
Don't remember what
being in love is like,
because it's been so very long.
And I'm afraid to give my heart to you,
to find out that I was wrong.
But the feelings that I am having for you,
are so very strong.
And The thought of waking up without you
seem so very wrong.
So, if I open up my heart to you,
Please don't you lead me on.

On Paper, I am Free

On paper I can open up and express,
whatever is on my mind.
Capturing all the things that I want to say,
Verbally, out loud.
But when I open up my mouth,
the words are so hard to find.
On paper, I am free,
no longer jailed within,
by all the emotions that I want to share,
verbally, but that are compressed in.
On paper, there is no shame, I am not shy.
But verbally, I tend to stray away
From all the emotions that are trapped inside.
On paper, I'm free to be me.
The person that lives within
But when it comes to expressing myself verbally,
That person remains locked in.
Verbally, I am a prisoner
to all the things that's, once spoken could set me free
so, I remain trapped by my own insecurities,
Only on Paper, Am I Free.

I Miss You

How can your mere words alone
bring so much joy to me?
How is it that I **miss you**,
when we have yet to meet?
How is it that I feel you,
when we have yet to Touch?
Never spent a day or night with you,
yet I miss you, oh, so much.
If I'm missing you now,
before we ever meet.
If I'm feeling you
before we ever touch.
How will I be able to let you go,
when I miss you now, so much?

Forehead Kisses

Your kisses on my forehead,
makes me feel like I am queen.
I sometimes have to pinch myself,
because it feels like I'm in a dream.
There's something about a forehead kiss,
that sends me almost spiraling out of control.
*A gentle kiss from **YOU** on my forehead,*
and chills, erupts throughout my soul.
It's the littleBig things, like forehead kisses,
that I reminisce about when we are apart,
the simplicity yet power of your Forehead Kisses
*is why **YOU** are forever embedded in my heart.*

I Want To…..

I want to stare into your eyes,
without either of us saying a word,
because it would be no need for us to talk,
for our hearts would have already heard.
I want to touch your face,
trace every inch of your cheeks
with your eyes close, savoring every second
slightly moaning because you're to choked up to speak.
I want to kiss your lips,
like you've never been kissed before.
Generating an electric spark,
that would keep you coming back for more.
I want to massage you, gently,
caressing your body from head to feet.
Stimulating you in unchartered areas,
beyond your wildest belief.
I want to hold you in my arms,
savoring the touch and feel of your skin.
Because I'm so captivated by your beauty,
that dwells from deep within.

Never Turning Back

Both of our lives have changed tremendously
and for me, I'm never looking back.
I'll reach for you and hold your hand,
if you get the urge to turn back.
I'll get behind you and give you a push,
if you feel you can't go on.
That backbone, then, I will become,
for when you are weak, I will be strong.
There're going to be times when my shoulder,
you might need to lean.
That's when I will show up strong
to support my lover and my best friend.
I will be there to pick you up,
if and when you fall.
I will be there to cushion your blow,
if you run into a brick wall.
We will always be there for each other,
my **twinMate***, you will always be.*
Both of us giving 100 % of ourselves,
the way relationships are supposed to be.
So if you get discourage,
search deep within your mind and heart.
For that is where you will always find me.
The place I've been from the very start.

If You Want Me

If you want me in your life,
like I want you,
just know that there are things
that I could never do.
I could never pretend that I'm ok,
if the pain has not gone away
so would you still love me
during those not so okay days?
At times I might shut down,
Due to all the pain, from my past,
I had endured,
Would you hold and comfort me?
Your love for me, reassured.
If you wanted me in your life,
then we must choose honesty over fear.
Be truthful about everything,
even if at times it causes tears.
If you want me in your life,
then to me, you must be true.
For I only have room for you in my heart
and I'll always be true to you.

When We Met

When I first saw you standing there,
I didn't want to let you out of my sight
and with just one stare into your eyes,
I just wanted to hug and hold you tight.
You had a smile that was perfect
and your stance demonstrated so much pride.
Standing next to you, I felt so comfortable,
I was beginning to feel all mushy inside.
When we meet, we were total strangers.
Yet, I believed I loved you before your face
I did see.
I didn't know what kind of man that you were
but you bought a sense of calmness around me.
I had no idea what a real man was
until you introduced yourself to me.
At that instant, I felt and knew
Instantaneously,
that I would love you for eternity.

If I Give You My Heart

If I give you my heart,
Something that I've never given
to anyone before,
would you return that love?
Or would you take my heart
and walk right out the door?
If I give you my heart,
with all the damages and hurt
it has sustained,
would you look past all my scars
And only see, all the love,
to you, that I would bring.
If I give you my heart,
Would you shield it from
any and all additional aches and pain?
Promising to love and protect me,
so that I won't ever be hurt and abused again.
If I Give You My Heart?

I Wonder

I wonder how often you think of me?
Seeing that we spend most of our time apart.
I wonder do you miss me?
Do you long for me in your heart?
I wonder do you close your eyes?
Imaging that I was there with you?
Right by your side, walking hand in hand.
Doing all the things that we love to do.
I wonder do you ever hear a song,
that makes you think of me?
And all the love that we have for each other,
And how happy, together, we'll always be.
I wonder have you ever saw someone,
that made you think of me?
Because they said or did something,
but in your eyes,
it was only I, that you could see.
I wonder do you think of me at night?
When you're getting in bed,
climbing between the sheets.
Wishing that I was right beside you,
that I was the last face that you saw,
before you fell asleep.
I Wonder?

If

If you take you away from us,
then I will be all alone.
If you walk out of my life,
all my hopes and dreams would be gone.
If you decide to leave me,
if you don't love me anymore,
my world would be turned upside down,
worse than it ever has been before.
If you refuse to talk to me,
ignore me, reject my touch
my heart, that I had given to you,
that you promise to protect,
would be crushed.
If I can no longer make you laugh,
if my jokes, you find a bore.
Tell we what I need to do,
before you walk out that door.

If you find it hard to talk to,
just know that I'm listening to.
So share with me what we need to do to fix us,
tell me what we need to do.
If you fall in love again,
I pray that other love, new woman is me.
I pray that each time we fight and make up
In love again, you will fall, and in your eyes,
I would be all you ever see.
If.

You Are

You are my refreshing shower in the summer time,
after a hot and sticky day.
Showering over my achy and sweaty body,
Washing all of the pain and aches away.
You are that full course meal,
When I haven't eaten for a week.
Only your touch can fulfill me,
Only then, will my hunger cease.
You are my sun when the sky is cloudy.
You brighten up my day.
That ray of light you generate
With the beautiful things, to me, you say.
You are that umbrella that shelters me,
Protecting me from the rain that steadily falls.
As long as your arms are around me,
I know I won't get wet at all.
You are my hopes and dreams for tomorrow,
and for the rest of life.
Like that umbilical cord that attaches a baby in its
mother's womb,
You're someone I can't do without.
You are my pillow, my blanket and bed,
The place where I lay my body down to rest at night.
So much comfort I feel as I snuggle near you,
With your arms around me, holding me tight.

You are my other half, my twinMate,
It's like we share the same heart.
No need for doctors to operate,
Because it would kill us if we are apart.
So I'll just stay attached to you, myLove
And never, no never shall we depart.

About the Author

Born in Gadsden, SC but has been living in Columbia, SC for over 40 years. Angela Hugee started writing at the age of 12 and over the years, her passion for writing continues to grow.

She is the mother of five children and grandmother of eight, which she considers all of them to be a gift from God. After all of her children were grown and gone, she decided to go back to school to obtain her GED. After obtaining her GED in 2009, she went on to receive an Associate Degree in Business from Strayer University in 2012, which she considers to be one of her biggest accomplishments.

Angela's passion and dream to one day become a published author never waived and In February of 2024 her 1ˢᵗ book, **Religious Poetry with Wings** was published and is available on Amazon.com.

Angela's motto in life is *"never say what you can't do, say I haven't learned it yet. Because when you keep your mind open to learning new things, with God, you can accomplish anything.*

Made in the USA
Columbia, SC
01 December 2024